MINERVA LOUISE
and the RED TRUCK

Janet Morgan Stoeke

DUTTON CHILDREN'S BOOKS · NEW YORK

Copyright © 2002 by Janet Morgan Stoeke
All rights reserved.

CIP Data is available.

Published in the United States 2002 by Dutton Children's Books,
a division of Penguin Putnam Books for Young Readers
345 Hudson Street, New York, New York 10014
www.penguinputnam.com
Designed by Jason Henry
First Edition • Printed in Hong Kong
1 3 5 7 9 10 8 6 4 2
ISBN 0-525-46909-5

For Barrett, with love

Minerva Louise loved the red truck.

It was one of her favorite places to play.

What's in here today? she wondered.

Oh, dress-up clothes! What fun!

And a big box full of toys.

Oh, look—a table and chairs.
Minerva Louise was so happy.

But right in the middle of her tea
party, she felt a bump and a jiggle.

She heard a *vroom!* And then she saw the fence moving away.

Minerva Louise was so excited.
She was going for a ride!

As they zoomed along, she saw all
kinds of things. A beautiful lake…

…farmers, hard at work in the fields…

…and a silly barn wearing a hat!

They came up over the hill, and Minerva
Louise saw a big field. It was full of trucks.

Wow, a truck farm. They are all having so much fun here!

Look at the little baby trucks
playing in the sand.

And the big trucks are showing off how strong they are.

There's a truck with a slide.
I love to slide.

Oh, there's even a swing.
What a wonderful place!

Almost as wonderful as home.

Minerva Louise loved seeing the new trucks.
But her favorite was still her own dear, red truck.

Wow! Except maybe *that* truck!
I want to ride on that truck next!